KEEKER

and the Sugar Shack

Book design by Mary Beth Fiorentino.
Typeset in Weiss Medium.
The illustrations in this book were rendered in pen and ink with
digital texture.
Manufactured in China.

Library of Congress Cataloging-in-Publication Data
Higginson, Hadley.
Keeker and the sugar shack / by Hadley Higginson ; illustrated by
Maja Andersen.
p. cm.
Summary: Upon learning that an older woman has moved into
the run-down, creepy Crab Apple Hill Farm, nine-year-old Keeker
rides her pony, Plum, over to find out whether the woman is
a witch.
ISBN-13: 978-0-8118-5455-9 (library ed.)
ISBN-10: 0-8118-5455-8 (library ed.)
ISBN-13: 978-0-8118-5456-6 (pbk.)
ISBN-10: 0-8118-5456-6 (pbk.)
[1. Ponies—Fiction. 2. Neighbors—Fiction. 3. Witches—Fiction.
4. Farm life—Vermont—Fiction. 5. Vermont—Fiction.]
I. Andersen, Maja, ill. II. Title.
PZ7.H534945Kef 2006
[E]—dc22
2005027124

Distributed in Canada by Raincoast Books
9050 Shaughnessy Street, Vancouver, British Columbia V6P 6E5

10 9 8 7 6 5 4 3 2

Chronicle Books LLC
680 Second Street, San Francisco, California 94107

www.chroniclekids.com

KEEKER

and the Sugar Shack

HADLEY HIGGINSON Illustrated by MAJA ANDERSEN

chronicle books · san francisco

Chapter 1

This is Catherine Corey Keegan Dana, but everyone calls her Keeker. Keeker lives in Vermont with her mom, her dad, five dogs, two cats, a goat, a parakeet, a hamster, a goldfish— and a pony named Plum.

Keeker is almost ten. Her pony, Plum, is nearly nine. But Plum is *so* bossy. You'd think she was the older one!

Every year as the snow melts and the rain sets in, Vermont gets very muddy. So muddy, in fact, that everyone calls it mud season.

During mud season, the dirt roads get thick and gooey. Cars get stuck. Trucks get stuck. Even tractors get stuck!

It's too muddy for Keeker and Plum to go riding, so Keeker has to stay indoors a lot. It wouldn't be so bad if she had brothers or sisters, but since she doesn't, it is SO boring. There isn't even anyone to play Yahtzee with.

Shluck-shluck-shluck—that's what it sounds like when Plum walks from one side of the field to the other.

No matter how many times Keeker suds her up and rinses her off, Plum still ends up with mud all the way up past her knees, like socks.

And every time Plum tries to dig around for some delicious grass, all she gets is . . . mud.

Plum is so bored that she's started chewing on the fence posts. Sometimes they give her lip splinters, but she doesn't care—at least it's something to do.

One Saturday after it had been raining a cold, dreary rain for what seemed like forever, the sun peeked out. Just a little.

Keeker was upstairs running around with panty hose on her head, pretending to have long braids like Laura Ingalls Wilder. Three of the dogs were wearing panty-hose hair, too.

"Mom!" yelled Keeker. "The sun is OUT! Can we go riding? Please? Please? Puh-LEEZE?"

"Well," said Mrs. Dana, "I'm not sure . . .
The horses are so dirty . . ."

But with Keeker wearing panty hose on her
head, it was hard to say no.

Mrs. Dana could tell that her daughter was
going to lose her marbles if she had to spend
even one more second inside.

"OK," said Mrs. Dana. "Go get your pony!"

"Yay!" said Keeker, and she hurried outside to catch Plum and bring her back to the barn.

"Finally!" thought Plum. Usually she tried to sneak out of going riding, but not today.

Mud season was so boring that even Plum was dying to go out.

Chapter
2

Keeker and her mom washed off Plum and Mrs.
Dana's big horse, Pansy. They put on saddles
and bridles, and the four of them set off down
the road. *Glop-glop-glop.*

"It's like riding through peanut butter!"
laughed Keeker.

"More like a nasty, marshy bog," grumped
Plum as she picked her way through the muck.

Plum had never actually SEEN a nasty, marshy bog, but she imagined it would be just like this.

It took them almost an hour to get to their nearest neighbor, the Doolan Dairy. The dairy was kind of stinky (lots of cows and cow pies), but Mr. Doolan himself was very nice (and smelled good—like green grass and pipe smoke).

Normally Mr. Doolan didn't say much, but on this day he rushed out of the house, waving his arms to talk to them.

"You'll NEVER believe it," said Mr. Doolan. "Someone bought Crab Apple Hill Farm!"

Crab Apple Hill Farm was an old falling-down house with an old falling-down barn. It sat by itself up on the hill, and for as long as Keeker could remember, it had been covered in brambles and scary looking.

"Who would want to live THERE?" Keeker
wondered. It gave her the creeps just thinking
about it.

"Yuck, crab apples," sniffed Plum. Crab apples
were small and sour and wormy. Plum preferred
the fat pink apples that grew on her tree.

Keeker had a million questions.

Who bought that old farm? Had they lived there long? What were they going to do up there? Didn't they care that it was scary? Did they have kids? Or horses?

Mr. Doolan leaned in close to Keeker. "All I know," he said, "is that it's a woman, probably about your grandma's age."

All alone on that old rundown farm? "No way," thought Keeker. "Weird."

That night the rain came back. It fell and fell and fell, clattering against the windowpanes like pebbles. The wind howled.

Keeker tossed and turned under her covers. Every time she tried to close her eyes and go to sleep, all she could picture was that creepy old house up on the hill.

She tried to imagine the old lady who lived there. And in Keeker's imagination, the old lady didn't look like her grandma. She looked like . . .

A witch.

Chapter
3

The next morning the rain had stopped. It was another almost-sunshiny day, and Keeker woke up with a plan. She knew exactly what she needed to do—investigate.

"Mom," she said, in her most sugary-sweet voice, "would it be OK if I take Plum out again? Can we go by ourselves this time? Please? Please? PLEASE?"

Mrs. Dana was always a little suspicious of the sugary-sweet voice.

"Well, OK," she said, after a pause. "As long as it doesn't rain."

When Keeker got down to the barn, Plum was standing out by her water trough, sunning herself. Her eyes were closed and her whiskers were twitching—she LOVED to sunbathe.

"Mmmmmm," sighed Plum. With her eyes closed, she could imagine it was summertime and the bees were buzzing lazily around the blackberry bushes.

She was so dreamily daydreaming, in fact,
she didn't even hear Keeker come up.

Keeker brushed Plum off as fast as she could.
It wasn't easy—Plum still had most of her thick
winter coat and was as woolly as a bear.

"Why are we in such a hurry?" Plum
grumped.

Keeker was busy muttering to herself.
"There's some weird old lady up there, and no
one even CARES! . . ."

"Plum," whispered Keeker, looking both ways
to make sure no one was around, "I think that

old lady up at Crab Apple Hill Farm might be a witch. I think it's up to us to check it out."

"A witch!" thought Plum. "Hmmph." She wasn't at all sure she wanted to go someplace called Crab Apple Hill Farm. Especially since it was such a good day for sunbathing.

Then again, it did sound a bit sneaky. And Plum loved to be sneaky.

As Keeker and Plum hurried down the road, there was only one thing on their minds: How would they get up to Crab Apple Hill without being seen?

"We should go through the woods," thought Plum. It was way too early for fiddleheads, but there might be some berries left over from last summer, hiding underneath the snow.

"Yum," thought Plum.

But Keeker had a better idea.

If they cut through Mr. Doolan's cow fields, they'd come out right behind the barn at Crab Apple Hill.

"Woo-hoo!" said Keeker out loud. She was trying to pump herself up so she wouldn't be scared.

"Boo," grumped Plum. If they went that way, there would be no berries. Only cow pies.

Keeker hopped off Plum and looked around to make sure no one was watching. Then she opened the gate to the cow pasture, led Plum in, and hopped back on.

Shluck-shluck-shluck. The cow field was WAY muddier than Plum's pasture; in fact, it was downright gross. And suddenly, they were surrounded by cows.

Plum was a little nervous. She didn't like all that hot cow breath.

"Shoo!" said Keeker, waving her crop at them. She didn't seem nervous at all.

Plum huffed and puffed as they climbed the hill. The cows didn't seem to mind. They mooed and bobbed their heads as Plum and Keeker trudged by.

Finally, they got to the top. And there, standing right in front of the path into the woods, was . . .

A bull. A big, mean-looking bull with a ring in his nose and everything.

Chapter

4

Keeker took a big deep breath. Her heart was whumping, and her mind was racing. What should she do? How would they get by that big old bull?

This had happened to her and her mom before when they'd been out riding, and her mom always just calmly rode around the bulls.

"OK, Plum," said Keeker. "Just ignore him. He won't bother us if we don't bother him."

They made a WIDE circle around the bull and hurried into the woods.

"Phew!" said Keeker. She was so relieved she felt as if she might faint.

"Dumb old bull," thought Plum. Now that they were past him, he didn't seem so scary.

They went just a little way, until they hit a falling-down stone wall. On the other side of the wall was the messiest, muddiest barnyard Keeker had ever seen.

Crab Apple Hill Farm.

"Surely only a witch would live here," Keeker
thought. She could just imagine all the spells
and potions bubbling away.

Keeker climbed off Plum and hunkered down
behind the stone wall. She tugged on the reins
to see if she could get Plum to hunker, too.

"Ponies don't bend like that," snorted Plum.

So instead, Keeker tried a disguise. She
picked some branches and tucked them into
Plum's bridle.

From where they were hunkering, Keeker
and Plum could clearly see the house, the barn
and, off to the side, a little falling-down shack.
The shack had a chimney with smoke coming
out of it. It had little tiny windows. It was too
small to be a house and way too small to be
a barn.

"Aha!" thought Keeker. There must be a cauldron in there, cooking over a fire. She thought
of some especially creepy witches she'd seen in
a play. "Bubble, bubble, toil and trouble . . ."

Suddenly—*scrrrrrreeeeeeeeeekkkk*—the screen
door at the back of the house swung open, and
an old lady came out carrying a kettle.

She had wild gray hair and was wearing a
kooky skirt and a couple of coats. A big hairy
dog snuffled along behind her.

Laughing and cackling, the old lady walked
right by where Keeker and Plum were hiding
and disappeared into the shack.

Keeker's heart started whumping again. Even Plum couldn't quite believe her eyes.

"She's totally a witch," whispered Keeker. "I've never seen anyone who looked so kooky! And did you see that dog? It was huge! I think it might have been . . . a woof!"

(Keeker had trouble saying her *l*s. She meant "a wolf.")

The old lady stayed in the shack for what
seemed like forever. Keeker's knees were wet,
and her back hurt from hunkering.

Plum was uncomfortable, too—the branches
in her bridle were starting to feel very poky.
And even though she didn't like to admit it, she
was very afraid of wolves.

Keeker began to think of all the scary stories she'd read, stories about kids alone in the woods with witches. What was that old lady DOING in there? What exactly was in that cauldron?

"Yikes," said Keeker softly to herself. Now she was really scared.

Even Plum started to shiver a little bit.

Just then—*scrrrrrreeeeeeeeeekkkk*—the crooked door on the shack swung open, and the old lady came out again, with the big dog right behind her.

She hurried past Plum and Keeker, humming to herself. But the big dog did NOT hurry past. In fact, it stopped right in front of Keeker and Plum.

"Oh, no," thought Keeker miserably. But it was too late. The big hairy dog was climbing over the falling-down wall and coming right for them.

"HELP!" Keeker shrieked, "WOOF! RUN!"

She grabbed Plum's reins and scrambled
over the wall, with Plum scrambling right
behind her.

They sprinted across the barnyard with the
huge woof panting behind them.

Chapter
5

Keeker had no choice but to dash inside the house, sliding on a rug and almost tumbling into the coat closet. Plum went clattering into the chicken coop, sending feathers flying (and making all the chickens flap and squawk).

The huge woof-dog skidded to a stop and began to lick its paws.

Inside the house, Keeker burst into the kitchen—and got the surprise of her life.

There, sitting at a little yellow table, was her mom. Eating pancakes.

"Keeker!" coughed Mrs. Dana, startled. "What on EARTH are you doing here?"

"Mom!" panted Keeker, "What are YOU doing here! Why are you eating PANCAKES at the WITCH HOUSE?"

Mrs. Dana just laughed. "Oh, Keeker. Honestly!"

"What's this about a witch?" said the old lady, coming through the kitchen door.

Up close, she didn't look very scary. Her kooky skirt had big flowers all over it, and she had pink cheeks and twinkly eyes.

"Ummm, Keeker, this is our new neighbor, Mavis Yardbottom," said Keeker's mom. "She's been making maple syrup, and she invited me over to taste the first batch."

"Pancakes, hon?" asked Mavis Yardbottom, bending over Keeker with a big stack of flapjacks.

Keeker felt very, very, very silly. Especially since the pancakes were delicious, and Mavis was as nice as she could be.

After they'd all had seconds and thirds (and rescued Plum from the henhouse), Mavis took them out to see the sugar shack.

"This is where the magic happens!" Mavis said happily. "This is where I boil the tree sap to make the maple syrup."

There was absolutely nothing scary in the sugar shack. Just vats of sap, bubbling away and turning into sweet-smelling syrup.

Since Plum hadn't gotten any pancakes, Mavis gave her a maple-sugar candy, which was just as good. The big dog got one, too.

"His name is Clancy," said Mavis, patting him on his hairy head. "Isn't he a sweetie?"

He was sweet. He didn't even mind when Plum nosed over and ate his candy, too.

That night it rained again. But it wasn't a cold, clattering kind of rain; it was more gentle. *Ping-ping-ping.*

Plum curled up in her stall, licking her lips. For once, there was no mud in her whiskers— just maple sugar. Keeker fell asleep with her hands still syrup-sticky. (As usual, she had only pretended to wash her hands before dinner.)

Up on the hill, the old falling-down house didn't look so scary anymore. Lamplight glowed in the windows. Mavis Yardbottom was tucked in under her favorite quilt, and next to her bed the big hairy dog snuffled and snored.

Smoke from the sugar shack spun up into the sky, blanketing the woods like cotton candy. Everyone slept soundly (and everyone's dreams were extra sweet).

3 1170 00776 3240

KEEKER

and the Springtime Surprise

Text © 2007 by Hadley Higginson.
Illustrations © 2007 by Lisa Perrett.

Series design by Kristine Brogno and Mary Beth Fiorentino.
Book design by Mariana Oldenburg.
Typeset in Weiss Medium.
The illustrations in this book were rendered Adobe Illustrator.
Manufactured in China.

Barbie is a registered trademark of Mattel, Inc.

Library of Congress Cataloging-in-Publication Data
Higginson, Hadley.
Keeker and the springtime surprise / by Hadley Higginson;
illustrated by Lisa Perrett.
p. cm.
Summary: It is springtime in Vermont, and new life abounds along
with new baby groundhogs in Plum's field, and knowing how her
father feels about them, ten-year-old Keeker decides to stage a
"Save the Groundhogs" event.
ISBN-13 978-0-8118-5598-3 (library edition)
ISBN-10 0-8118-5598-8 (library edition)
ISBN-13 978-0-8118-5599-0 (pbk.)
ISBN-10 0-8118-5598-6 (pbk.)
[1. Farm life—Vermont—Fiction. 2. Animals—Infancy—Fiction.
3. Ponies—Fiction. 4. Theater—Fiction.]
I. Perrett, Lisa, ill. II. Title.
PZ7.53499Keek 2007
[E]—dc22
2006021106

Distributed in Canada by Raincoast Books
9050 Shaughnessy Street, Vancouver, British Columbia V6P 6E5

10 9 8 7 6 5 4 3 2 1

Chronicle Books LLC
680 Second Street, San Francisco, California 94107

www.chroniclekids.com

KEEKER

and the Springtime Surprise

by **HADLEY HIGGINSON** Illustrated by **LISA PERRETT**

chronicle books · san francisco

Chapter
1

This is Catherine Corey Keegan Dana, but everyone calls her Keeker. Keeker is ten. She lives in Vermont with her parents and a kazillion pets: five dogs, four cats, two hamsters, a goat, a goldfish, and a baby bird named Peep.

There's one big horse on Keeker's farm. And one very small (and sometimes sneaky) pony named Plum.

Springtime in Vermont can be quite surprising.
When the snow finally melts, all sorts of things
that have been hidden all year suddenly turn up.

The dogs find their old tennis balls. Keeker sometimes finds a lost Barbie doll or a toy tractor. And Plum often finds a halter that's been left on the ground by someone who was in a big hurry to go riding.

The other fun thing about spring is that there are baby animals just about everywhere. In fact, Keeker found Peep just sitting on the lawn, right next to her broken nest, peeping her head off.

Two of the dogs were sniffing around her, wondering what all the fuss was about.

"Oh, CUTE!" said Keeker, when she saw Peep. She picked her up very, very carefully and carried her inside.

Keeker's mom knew exactly what to do.

"That's a cedar waxwing," said Mrs. Dana. "They usually eat berries and bugs, so I think if we feed her some fruit and a little bit of meat, she'll be fine."

They made a home for Peep in Keeker's bathroom and fed her teeny tiny bits of raw hamburger and cut-up grapes.

The baby bird was as happy as she could be. She hopped around the bathroom, peeping at Keeker and pooping all over the place.

Keeker wasn't the only one with a new animal to take care of. A mama groundhog and six roly-poly groundhog babies had made a home in Plum's pasture.

This made Plum VERY nervous. She knew that Keeker's dad didn't like groundhogs at all; he always yelled and waved his arms at them.

(He wasn't trying to be mean; he just wanted to shoo them away. Groundhogs make holes in the ground that the horses can trip in.)

Plum didn't mind the holes, though. And she liked seeing Mrs. Groundhog and her pups waddling across the field.

But what to do about Mr. Dana?

"I wish they'd wait till after dark to strut around," thought Plum anxiously.

But Mrs. Groundhog was bold as brass. She paraded her babies in the bright light of day, not caring who saw them.

It was too worrisome. Plum needed to do something.

So every time the groundhogs went out, Plum went with them. She walked right next to

them, so that from the Danas' kitchen window, you couldn't see any pups.

"La dee da da," pretended Plum. "No ground-hogs here!"

The groundhog babies didn't mind at all. They were cool and comfortable walking in Plum's shadow, and they liked it when her tail tickled their heads.

Of course, hiding something from Mr. Dana was one thing; hiding something from Keeker was quite another. Keeker noticed the ground-hog babies right away.

"Oh, WOW!" she said when she saw them.
"Even Dad couldn't be mad at *these* groundhogs.
I'll get Mom to talk to him."

Keeker galloped off to find her mom.

Chapter

2

She looked all over the house—upstairs, downstairs, in the basement, and even in the garage. She looked in the vegetable garden and out in the shed. She checked down by the pond. Finally, Keeker just stood in the back-yard and hollered.

"MOOOOOOMMMM!" yelled Keeker.

"WHAAAAAAAT?" Mrs. Dana yelled back.

She was in the barn with Doc Thomas, the vet who took care of the animals at Keeker's house. Keeker's mom and Doc Thomas were standing outside of Pansy's stall, talking very seriously about something.

They didn't even notice when Keeker came up and didn't pay any attention when Keeker tugged on Mrs. Dana's sleeve or jiggled her elbow.

"MOOOOOOMMMM!" said Keeker.

"KEEKER!" said Mrs. Dana. "Honestly. What is it?"

"I want to SHOW you something," said Keeker. By this time, she was hopping back and forth from one foot to another because she just couldn't wait any longer. She knew her mom would love those fat baby groundhogs!

"Well, I'm sorry," said Mrs. Dana, "but I'm very busy right now. Pansy is due to have her foal any day now, and Doc and I need to make sure everything is ready."

Mrs. Dana's horse was going to have a baby (a foal is a baby horse), and that was all anyone talked about. Pansy, Pansy, Pansy. Keeker was sick of it! What about her? What about Plum?

Hmmmph. Keeker stopped hopping.

Since her mom was being no fun at all, Keeker went off to find her dad.

She found him outside his woodshop, standing in a big pile of lumber and looking frazzled. Goatie was rummaging around in the toolbox, seeing if there was anything in it that would be fun to eat.

"Dad!" said Keeker. "I have something really cool to show you. I know you THINK you

don't like groundhogs, but these are little baby ones, and they're really cute and . . ."

"Not now, Keeker," said Mr. Dana, sounding exasperated. I'm really busy. I need to work on Pansy's stall, and I don't want to talk to you about groundhogs. You know that they dig holes! If you show them to me, I'm just going to have to chase them away."

WHAT? Chase them away? They were so little—and so cute! Just thinking about it made Keeker want to cry.

Keeker lay down on the ground and worked up a gigantic tantrum.

"Oh, poor little baby groundhogs!" she sobbed, flailing her arms around.

Mr. Dana was not impressed. He just frowned and kept on hammering. Eventually, Keeker got tired of weeping and moaning, so she picked herself up and stomped off.

Keeker felt very cranky. Stupid Pansy and her stupid foal. It wasn't fair! Keeker went over to Plum's field and sat down under the apple tree, scratching her back against the bark the way Plum sometimes did.

"Nobody even CARES about us," said Keeker to Plum. "Everyone's all bothered about Pansy. I

bet we could run away, and no one would even notice."

Plum looked at Keeker suspiciously. Running away sounded like a lot of work. Plus, Plum had her groundhogs to take care of.

Keeker lay down in Plum's field and looked up. The clouds rolled and tumbled by, changing shape as they went. They looked like clowns. Or characters in a play.

A play. What an idea! A big, fancy play, with costumes and everything. That would impress her parents and give Keeker the perfect opportunity to ask for a favor. Keeker could see it now: her parents applauding and clapping, Keeker and Plum taking a bow, and then Keeker saying (rather grandly, of course), "This magnificent theatrical production was brought to you by the groundhogs. Save the groundhogs!"

A play would be just the ticket. It would help save the pups, and it would get everyone to forget about Pansy and the new foal, at least for a little while.

Chapter

3

Keeker was so excited she felt like she might explode. Instead, she ran over to Plum and hugged her hard around the neck.

"Won't this be cool?" said Keeker to Plum. "We can make costumes and everything."

"Gak!" snorted Plum. "Stop strangling me, you crazy girl."

But secretly, Plum thought it was brilliant.

Of course, the big question was: Which play should they do? Keeker thought of some stories she knew. "Cinderella." "Sleeping Beauty." "Snow White and the Seven Dwarfs." Blah. They all seemed babyish. Plus, there were no good pony parts.

Keeker decided to go dig in her parents'
library for inspiration. She ran back to the
house and got Peep and let her perch on her
shoulder. (Peep LOVED excursions to other
rooms.) They headed downstairs to the library.

The library was one of those rooms that
Keeker's mom liked to keep tidy, so usually

the door was shut (to keep the dogs out—and
quite possibly to keep Keeker out, too!).

Keeker always felt like she should be quiet
in the library, even though there was no one
in there to tell her to "shush." She tiptoed in
and started looking through the books on the
lowest shelves.

Most of them were big and heavy and had lots of pictures. Keeker started flipping through a world atlas, admiring all the cities and states and oceans and islands. Especially islands.

"Hmmm," murmured Keeker, "maybe we should do a play about pirates!"

Peep peeped at that. She was sure she would make an *excellent* pirate parrot!

But then again, it was very hard to fake an ocean. A land play would be better.

On the very top shelf, the books were very old—and very dusty. Most had cracked leather bindings and funny titles. Keeker climbed up on the back of the couch so she could see better.

At the end of the shelf was a BIG book, with its title in gold: *Don Quixote, Man of La Mancha.*

Don Kee-Ho-Tay. Keeker had heard of him! From what she remembered, he was kind of

like a knight, except that he fought windmills
instead of dragons.

And, of course, he rode a horse. Perfect!

Keeker put Peep back in the bathroom and
ran outside to find Plum. Plum was standing in
the middle of the field—with her nose down a
groundhog hole.

Plum hadn't seen the groundhog pups all day,
and she was a little anxious.

"Where are they?" she wondered.

She sniffed and sniffed, but didn't smell any
groundhog smells. All she smelled was dark dirt
and grass roots. (And actually, it smelled quite
delicious!) "I could stay here all day," sighed
Plum.

Keeker left Plum to her sniffing (and groundhog spying), and went off to work on costumes.

Chapter 4

In the Don Quixote book, the clothes looked very old-timey. In fact, Don himself wore armor, like a medieval knight. But where in the world would Keeker find armor?

Just then, there was a loud CRASH. Keeker looked out the window and saw Goatie rooting around in the garbage cans. (Goatie LOVED garbage. He especially loved knocking

things over to get to it.) That gave Keeker a
fabulous idea.

Hmmm, maybe trash can lids would work?

Keeker went outside and found two lids. She
tied them together with some twine and hung
the whole thing over her head—and it looked
pretty great! It didn't look very royal, though.
And that Don Quixote guy thought a lot of
himself. . . .

"I need some feathers," thought Keeker. "Or something fancy. . . ."

Finding feathers turned out to be easy. There was a big pink feather duster in the kitchen closet. Keeker glued it onto her riding helmet. It looked MARVELOUS.

But what to do about Plum's costume? Because, of course, she needed one, too.

In the book, the horses all wore big drapey things under their saddles—things with tassels and stuff along the bottom. Things that looked an awful lot like . . . bedspreads!

Keeker trotted into her parents' bedroom and grabbed the bedspread. It had a fringe and everything. It was just right!

As for where the play would actually happen, well, that was obvious—Plum's field. In the book, Don Quixote liked to charge at windmills. Keeker and Plum could charge the apple tree.

Keeker dragged all the kitchen chairs down to the field, so her audience would have a place to sit. Then she hopped on Plum's back and went off to find her parents (to tell them all about the wonderful, amazing, spectacular play they were about to see).

Keeker and Plum clomped up onto the lawn, and Keeker yelled for her parents.

"MOOOMM! DAAAAADDD!"

No answer.

Plum took advantage of being up on the lawn by eating some daffodils. She loved it when Keeker rode her bareback. It was so much easier to get away with things.

After clomping all over the place for
almost an hour, Keeker and Plum finally found
Keeker's parents. They were in the barn again
(of course), all crowded around Pansy's stall

with Doc Thomas. GOSH. Couldn't they stop thinking about Pansy, even for just one minute?

Plum hoped being pregnant wasn't something you could catch, like a cold. She gave a little cough to see if she felt sick. (She didn't.)

"Mom! Dad!" said Keeker. "You HAVE to come down to Plum's field in about an hour

because we have a big surprise for you. You'll come, right? You promise?"

"Ummm, sure," said Keeker's mom, looking at a chart Doc Thomas was holding.

"Of course, Keeker," said Keeker's dad, waving his hand kind of absentmindedly.

Keeker sighed. Parents could be so difficult.

Chapter

5

Keeker and Plum hurried back down to Plum's field and began to get ready. First, Keeker tied on the garbage can lids, to make her clanky armor, and put on her feathered riding hat.

Then she used a marker to draw a very grand and curly mustache on herself. Voilá!

Plum's costume was easy. All Keeker had to do was drape the bedspread over Plum's back.

It didn't seem quite right, though. Something was missing . . . so Keeker drew a mustache on Plum, too.

Everything was ready. It was time to put on the play and save the groundhogs! Keeker

decided to hide the groundhogs in the hollow part of Plum's apple tree. Then at the end of the play (when everyone was wildly clapping and cheering), she would come out and say, "This play is dedicated to our WONDERFUL groundhog family."

Then the groundhogs would waddle out, and her parents would fall in love with them, and everything would be fine. It was a fool-proof plan.

Plum stuck her nose down one of the groundhog holes and snorted as loud as she could. She did that a few more times, and eventually Mrs. Groundhog and all her babies came hurrying out of the other hole, looking grumpy.

Plum used her nose to very gently herd them over to the apple tree.

Keeker looked at her watch—it was almost showtime! She and Plum practiced charging a few times (Keeker used a broom instead of a lance) and then went behind the apple tree to wait for their audience.

They waited. And waited, and waited, and waited. Where WERE they? The groundhogs had all fallen asleep in a big furry pile. (It was very dark and cozy inside the apple tree.) And

even Plum was getting a little snoozy. (It was very comfortable under the bedspread.)

"Sheesh," said Keeker. "This is getting ridiculous. Come on, Plum."

Keeker stuck her lance (er, broomstick) in the air and gave Plum a mighty kick. Plum reared up a bit, making the bedspread flap impressively.

And they charged up to the barn. The groundhogs woke up with a start, came tumbling out of the apple tree, and waddled right after them!

"Ta-da ta-dum! Behold Don Quixote!" yelled Keeker, as they clattered (and flapped and

clanked) into the barn. But it was so, so quiet in there that she immediately felt weird. It was like the "shush" feeling in the library!

Keeker's parents and Doc Thomas were all in Pansy's stall. Keeker and Plum tiptoed down there and peeked over the edge of the door. Mrs. Groundhog and all the pups tiptoed down, too, and snuck *under* the stall door (where there was a nice big crack—just right for sneaking).

Pansy was standing quietly in the corner. All the grown-ups were clustered around her. And standing right in the middle was . . . the cutest, spindliest, sweetest-looking brand-new baby horse, still covered in goo and looking very wobbly on her legs.

"Ohhhhh," said Keeker.

"Wowie," thought Plum.

"Squeak!" squeaked the groundhogs. They were very impressed.

"Hey, you two," said Keeker's mom happily. "Say hello to Rosie—Pansy's very first foal!"

"Isn't she a beauty?" said Mr. Dana. He sounded a little choked up. Plum realized this was the perfect time to introduce the *other* babies. She stamped her foot a little, and Mr. Dana looked down and saw all six groundhog pups piled up and looked as sweet as can be.

Mrs. Groundhog felt very proud. Her babies were so well behaved!

Mr. Dana bent down with a big smile on his face. "Well, you guys are pretty cute, too," he said. And after that, Plum and Keeker figured the groundhogs would probably be okay. Phew!

"Hmmmm," said Mr. Dana. Keeker just *knew* he was thinking about groundhog holes.

"Don't worry, Dad," said Keeker. "I know what to do. Let's move the whole groundhog family to the field behind the barn. It's not used for horses anymore, so they can dig all the holes they want!"

Mr. Dana thought it was a great idea. He asked Keeker to lead Plum into the field, so the groundhogs would follow.

The field behind the barn was overgrown,
with lots of long grass and all kinds of wild-
flowers—daisies, clover, cornflowers, and even
black-eyed Susans.

Mrs. Groundhog loved it right away. So did
her pups—as soon as they were inside the gate,
they went squeaking off in different directions
to explore their new home.

Plum was *very* relieved. So was Keeker.

The whole rest of the day, Keeker and her parents stayed in the barn, watching Rosie and giving Pansy lots of treats and kisses. Plum hung around, too, in case anyone wanted to give *her* any treats. "After all," thought Plum, "Pansy isn't the only one who's had a busy day!"

For dinner, Keeker's mom put together a picnic basket and brought it down to the barn. Pretty soon it was bedtime—but no one felt like going back to the house.

"We could just camp out down here tonight,"
suggested Keeker's dad. "And Plum could stay in
her stall instead of going back down to the field."

"Well," thought Plum. "I suppose I could hang
around for a bit . . ."

Keeker and her mom and dad put hay bales
together to make two big beds. Then they
piled a ton of blankets and sleeping bags on top.
Camping in the barn was so fun!

Plum decided to sleep standing up so she could keep an eye on Rosie. (Rosie was kind of cute, after all.)

Rosie curled up next to her delicious warm-smelling mother. And in the field behind the barn, the groundhogs dug a comfy hole and pig-piled on top of each other.

All over Vermont, mamas and babies were snuggled up tight. The flowers in the field closed up their petals. And the big quiet earth rocked them all to sleep.

GALLOPING YOUR WAY IN FALL 2007

Introducing a new adventure in the Sneaky Pony series

KEEKER

and the Pony Camp Catastrophe

Keeker and Plum are SO excited! They get to go to sleepaway camp for girls and their ponies for a whole week. When they arrive, Keeker is pleased to discover that Camp Kickapoo looks just as she expected. Fun soon turns to frustration when Keeker's group gets stuck learning riding techniques that Keeker thinks are way too babyish. But when another camper's spirited pony bolts, Keeker and her friends prove that they can handle difficult riding challenges.